THE MISSING BRANCH

Bulwark Anthology
Volume Five

KAY MACLEOD

CONTENTS

1	CHAPTER ONE	1
2	CHAPTER TWO	5
3	CHAPTER THREE	13
4	CHAPTER FOUR	23
5	CHAPTER FIVE	27
6	CHAPTER SIX	35
7	CHAPTER SEVEN	45
8	CHAPTER EIGHT	51
9	CHAPTER NINE	59
10	CHAPTER TEN	67
11	CHAPTER ELEVEN	77
12	CHAPTER TWELVE	81
13	EPILOGUE	91

1

CHAPTER ONE

Stylistic curves stretched over the entirety of the wall. They were traced onto pieces of printer paper and held in place with Blu Tack at the minute, but the paint was there ready for the final piece. New sable-tipped brushes sat on the antique set of drawers, eager to be put to use.

Izzie rested her palm over the sheet that held her own name, her place in the intricate tapestry. It was penned with almost immaculate calligraphy, she still had some practice to put in before she committed to the final mural. She let her gaze rove over the sprawl of names; Michael, Louisa, Harry, Amanda. She knew each one and part of their unique story, even if just about a job or marriage. Each path meandered and split, adding more to the vast tale that made up who she was and where she'd come from.

The pale gap grinned at her. It was set back and off to the side, a sudden cutoff in the mid-1700s that refused to give up its secrets to her thorough research. It wasn't like she hadn't tried. Hours of Google searches and dozens of email requests for information hadn't turned up anything. It was like the family that had moved from England to America had just disappeared. She'd ruled out shipwreck; the Government didn't keep ship records of immigration that long ago, but there were indexes and compilations that confirmed her distant relations had made it there safely. It spelt out their destination. Then nothing.

Izzie grabbed her mug of tea from the top of the drawers, the liquid leaving fuzz on her tongue as she sipped at the almost too hot liquid. It ran down her throat and perfectly warmed her core. The cup left behind a ring on the folded sheet she'd plonked it on. She should be framing that instead of using it as a coaster. Her copy of the two weeks' notice she'd handed into the boss a fortnight ago, she slid it open to check for the hundredth time that she was really free. No more drudgery, no more tedious office chores.

Izzie was ready for an adventure.

After spending ten hours on a plane, the journey felt more like a slog. Once she'd made it out of the airport, Izzie dragged her little trundle luggage into her reasonably priced rental car and set off with a can of sickly sweet energy drink at her side and a post-it note with massive letters saying 'Stay On The Right!!!!' stuck firmly to the centre of the steering wheel.

Was she completely mental to do this? Ditch her job and travel halfway across the world with no proper plan, all alone… Izzie had a month here. Four weeks with nothing but her clothes and credit card, she hadn't booked hotels or sought attractions. Even she didn't know where her research would take her. Her parents hadn't liked the idea, not a single part of it. There had been more than one blistering argument.

But she knew that she had to know. The small gap was a gaping chasm, an imperfection on her grand project. Once Izzie filled that space, she would finally have the complete picture of herself - her history, and meaning, and purpose. For some reason, this part of the family was the most important part of the story. The feeling was impossible to pin down, but it intensified with every minute closer she got to the little town of Bulwark.

2

CHAPTER TWO

"Are you sure?" Izzie asked, trying to fight back the swell of panic in her chest.

"We got two rooms. Both are booked for the week, you want me to reserve you one for next Monday?" The woman readjusted her glasses on the wide bridge of her nose and whipped out a crumpled notebook from her back pocket, complete with a finger-length pencil crammed into the ring binding.

"I… I guess I'm not sure how long I'll be here," Izzie replied. "I might be moving on soon, depending on what I find."

"You won't be finding much in this town." The woman's face crinkled with a peal of laughter. "I reckon you're vacationing in the wrong place, miss. Nothing ever happens in Bulwark. You'll be much better off heading on over to one of the cities or take a trip down to Florida, they got plenty for you to see."

"I'm not really a theme park kind of girl. Actually, I'm here for historical research."

"Well, there's certainly some Civil War relics around, there was a battleground here, you see…"

"It's more specific," Izzie cut in, sensing an hour-long ramble oncoming, "I need records, genealogies, anything I can get my hands on about the area around 1760. Ah, but mostly I need a place to stay."

"Well, good luck with all that. Remember, Florida is a good back up plan." The woman shrugged and turned away, clearly dismissing her. This place was about to get a seriously crappy review if they showed up on TripAdvisor.

The door clattered shut as Izzie let it swing closed behind her. It would have been easy to miss the tiny sign proclaiming the building to be a hostel if she hadn't been scrutinising every structure for a chance that she'd be welcome there. One other place had apparently been closed for repairs. This town was not a hot tourist destination. Somehow that endeared her. Made her want to breach the defences of this closed off blip on the map and announce her presence in a way that they couldn't ignore.

The flutter of nerves faded with the thrum of the rental car's engine. Izzie was starting to get used to the sounds it made and the feel of the seat hugging her back. She pulled away from the useless hostel and resumed her trawl.

The situation was hardly dire; she had money and a car, the weather was way nicer here than back home, and the radio had some decent tunes to crank up as she drove. She belted out the choruses and other odd snatches of lyrics she knew and canvassed the last few streets, bobbing her head along to the drum beat.

Suddenly she was thrown forward, the car jolting to a stop.

Don't tell me it's broken down already.

But it hadn't. Izzie peered down to see her own foot jamming the brake pedal into the crumb-covered, threadbare mat. She'd stopped the car herself. Switching off the engine, Izzie ran a hand through her hair and inhaled a deep breath filled with the must of a dozen previous drivers. Damn, she must be super tired. Too much travelling, that was all.

A small road meandered off away from the town where she'd brought the vehicle to a halt. Izzie necked the last quarter of her energy drink, then plucked up the courage to drive a couple of meters to pull the car over and park it up neatly out of the way of oncoming traffic.

Next time she did this she'd book a room for the first night. Her body itched with the sour sweat of travel and she already felt overdressed in her jeans and long-sleeved tee. Just a quick walk to clear her head, then she'd get back to her exploration. Surely someone would put her up for the night. It was that or the back seat of the car.

The sun had moved. The shadows were different. The residences and rickety shop fronts of the town had been replaced by a thicket of trees. They seemed to shade her from the disinterest of the townsfolk, wrapping their branches around to direct her towards the centre of the road.

Izzie blinked rapidly, snatching glances left and right to make sense of where she was. Her perception was wrong, time and space didn't mean anything. She jammed the heels of her hands into the crusty dryness clinging to her eyelids. But she wasn't scared. She was empowered. There was nowhere safer than this single spot. She knelt in absolute wonder, the dampness of the sodden earth soaking into her jeans.

The puddle spread out in front of her rippled with a green almost toxic sheen, but she instinctively knew it wasn't. It was a shield and a cushion, a beautiful lake meant only to preserve life. A bubble floated to the surface and popped, releasing a bold, earthy scent that set her nostrils tingling. Her hand hovered a finger's breadth from the surface, trembling with the urge to be plunged in. She needed to know the consistency, whether the viscous liquid would cling to her skin or run down and off her fingertips. She wanted to take in the heady perfume again.

An abandoned car violated the pool, sunken into the centre with the door askew where the clumsy driver had managed to break free. Izzie wished she could wade in and pull it out. While she was this close to the goo, she almost believed she could.

Okay, this was properly, properly mad. She dragged herself upright, attempting to scrape off the mud pressed into her trousers. There went any chance of a friendly local letting her borrow their spare room for a night or two.

A rustle to her right grabbed Izzie's attention. A pair of luminous yellow eyes met her own.

Was that a wolf?

They weren't supposed to live around here, were they? Her mind threw up all the little snippets of information she'd read about the area. None could refute the shaggy, grey shape inching towards her. Its whole muzzle twitched as it breathed in her scent. A heavy paw squelched into the edge of the muddy patch.

The pool is shrinking… Izzie had no idea why the thought left her so forlorn. Or why she still didn't feel any fear. She'd always been the kind of kid that ran up to strange dogs and tried to pet them when her parents weren't looking, this wasn't Mrs Lowe's spaniel though. This was a predator.

The wolf took another step, head cocked to one side like it was trying to figure out what she was by listening to her body's rhythms. Izzie's hand was stretched out towards it. She didn't move it. It just was. The creature was huge. It could have easily taken down one of the bucks that roamed the tree line at the edge of her home village.

Another step. The wolf's flank heaved in time with Izzie's own breathing. In, out, in, out. She watched the ribcage expand and contract, not sure which of them led and which followed.

Step. The powerful neck stretched out, bringing the dagger-sharp fangs towards Izzie's flesh. A smudge of cold dampness brushed her palm as the wolf nuzzled her, then fled back into the wilderness.

"What just...?" She murmured at the scuff of retreating paws on grass.

Damn, this day just got weirder.

3

CHAPTER THREE

Back at the car, Izzie unlocked her suitcase and pulled back the clips. Tossing aside underwear and shorts, she finally found a light pair of leggings. After a quick scan to make sure there were no creepers, she peeled off the sodden jeans from her tacky skin and jammed on the clean clothing.

Okay, time to take stock. She was alone with no place to stay in an area with dangerous wild animals. Maybe that just made the experience more interesting? It would make a great story when she got home. If only she'd managed to take a photo!

Grinning, Izzie slammed her foot down on the throttle and took off back into town. Touched a wolf. Wow.

A half hour later she was still squirming in her seat with excitement, even with the complete blank on the place to stay. People barely offered her any help, pointing out the places she'd already checked or giving her a cool shrug. They seemed wary and taken aback by her. Like she was the boss's daughter, and they didn't want to be near her long enough to give any reason for her to take offence.

One of the last streets she needed to check blessed her with a better find. Bulwark's library. The sole reason she was even in the country. They must have some physical records here. Some kind of paperwork that could close that infuriating gap on her mural.

Warmth pooled around Izzie as she stepped out of the air-conditioned vehicle and slammed the door behind her. She looked up at the double storey building, taking in the old brickwork with peeling paintwork. A swift glance at the opening times billboard told her she was in luck.

Pushing into the entryway, Izzie took a second to absorb the stillness and incredible peace that washed over her. A library was the same wherever in the world it was. One of her favourite stories said they were all connected in some way, that books had a magic of their own and could communicate across time and space.

Beyond the tiny entrance hall, a rickety desk was set up. It was precariously bowed with the weight of piles of books, leaflets, and papers. The woman curled up in the armchair behind it didn't seem concerned. She'd removed her shoes and tucked her legs beneath her, and she was greedily consuming a book with a topless man on the front that looked like he picked up a lot of heavy weights.

"Excuse me…" Izzie whispered, half from the unspoken library rule and half because she hated interrupting a good read.

The woman's chin tilted up, her eyes still glued to the words momentarily as she finished her line.

"Oh!" She blinked rapidly and jumped to her feet, almost tipping herself headfirst into the desk as she flustered to get upright. "Sorry there, Ma'am. Been a quiet… year, ya know?"

"No problem whatsoever." Izzie gave a reassuring smile - finally, someone friendly. "I was hoping you guys had some old records here I could take a look at? I'm working out my family history and I've come to a bit of a dead end with what I could find online."

"We got all kinds of old junk and the like, second floor you'll find what you need. Can't be taking out any of those things but you're sure welcome to spend what time you need up there."

"Thank you so much, you've no idea how much I've been struggling to find my way around. I really could do with a hotel or bed-and-breakfast or something too. Do you know anywhere in town I could spend a few nights while I do my research?"

"We've got Google on the computers up there too, you can go take a look see if anything's around here. We don't tend to get much in the way of visitors, you probably noticed." The librarian's polished nails played with the corner of the next page of her novel.

"I'm sure I'll figure something out…" Izzie tiptoed past, doubtful the woman even noticed her as she plunged back into the steamy romance. Maybe she'd be able to recommend something for Izzie to read during the evenings here, it had been too long since she'd read for pleasure instead of tracking down ancestors.

Tatty bookcases made a maze of the ground floor, trying to distract her with their bountiful shelves. A few ancient chairs decorated the corners, each more worn than the last until one was covered with more patches than original fabric. Right over in the back corner, a narrow staircase led up to the next floor. A hand-written sign stuck to the wall read 'Computers' and had an arrow pointing up. Guess the records didn't need pointing out; technology would always be more popular than hundreds of years old paperwork. Not surprising, most people didn't even like modern paperwork.

The steps were unexpectedly sturdy, not uttering a single creak as Izzie ascended. The ancient bannister was polished smooth under her palm from the thousands of other knowledge seekers that must have climbed these stairs at some point in time. She stepped out past a 'No Eating' sign into an open space and blinked. The Bulwark Library computer suite was made up of four machines, two still with old fashioned bulky monitors. They were arranged in a square in the centre of the room on the kind of tables you'd find in a low-budget classroom.

The only other person up here was a guy slouched behind one of the slightly more up-to-date PCs. Izzie couldn't see much of him behind the giant screens, but he'd pulled one of the other chairs over and propped his lanky legs on it. He didn't glance up as she walked out into the room, just stayed intent on typing something on his keyboard. Maybe he'd be more receptive to some questioning in a little while if she left him to his work for now.

Cabinets and shelving took up most of the wall space, each piece of furniture uniquely clunky. A couple of desks were set apart from the computers, complete with a rickety former dining room chair and a pot filled with pens, pencils, rulers, and other odds and ends of stationary. Guess this would be her office for the next few days. Maybe the librarian wouldn't notice if she bunked down here for the night…

The first acre-deep drawer she pulled open at random let out a horrendous screech, Izzie winced and shot a glance at the guy. He didn't look back, but he did rustle around in a bag and pull out some crisps to nibble on.

"Hey, says 'no eating' over there," Izzie said with a smile to show she didn't particularly care, she just wanted to make the first contact.

"I ain't eating," he replied, taking another bite without looking at her. "I'm snacking."

Izzie couldn't help but grin at his thick accent and wonder if he was curious about hers. With the ice broken, she tiptoed over to stand next to him.

"Would the librarian agree with that?" She asked, hoping the bright cartoon character decorating his top meant that he had a decent sense of humour.

"Well, she'd have to come up here to disagree and that is something I doubt she's done since she got this job. So…" He shrugged and finally flickered a glance her way from under a thick, fringe of almost-black hair that brushed against his eyelashes. Izzie noticed the same hesitation twitch at his jaw that she'd seen in the other townspeople. For some reason, it wrenched at her stomach this time, like with him it should be different. Maybe because the lady downstairs had seemed slightly more open. Book people should be her people, but this guy could just be here for the computer.

"Don't get many visitors to this town, huh?" Izzie felt the desperation crack her voice and was instantly ashamed, she didn't want him to think she was looking for pity.

"Nope." His fingers fluttered at the keys, he was clearly impatient to be rid of her. The dark sleeves of his top reached past his wrists, but Izzie could see little spatters of red, raised skin on the backs of his hands like angry freckles.

"What did you do to your hands?"

He captured her with his eyes properly this time, pale grey pools that roved her features in a way that left her thoughts tripping over themselves as she wondered if she'd been too nosy. What if he'd been attacked? Or abused in some way? It was hardly any of her business to ask. She still wanted to know, had the urge to dig deeper. Bulwark would give her something, damn it.

"Why?" He asked.

"Because… I dunno. Honestly, I'm just making conversation. I'm going to be here a while and I could use a hand getting to know the place."

"You moved here?" There was a reluctance in his tone still, but surely this was progress.

"I'm in the country for a month, for research." Izzie grabbed her phone and opened up her photos, showing him the shots of her mural in progress. "This is what I'm working on, see? Back here is where the sister of my many-great grandma emigrated from England to America. She came with her husband and they were supposed to have moved here but I can't find anything about them or their descendants. I'm hoping to uncover something in the records here."

Too late she remembered that no-one else ever got as excited about genealogy as she did. She looked over, expecting to see the same glazed over expression that her friends and family always wore when she showed off her latest find. But he was fixated on the photo, he reached over and pinched the screen to zoom in.

"You write those all out?"

"I did…"

"Nice calligraphy." Those two words validated hours of practice, Izzie wondered if he could ever comprehend how much that compliment meant to her. "Not sure how much you'll find here, even in a month. Tessa ain't one for keeping much order in the place."

"Then I suppose I'd better get started."

"I suppose you had." He quickly hit the X in the corner of his webpage and logged out of the PC, then grabbed a backpack from under the desk. He pulled out another packet of crisps and left them on the side. "If Tess catches you, say you're snacking, not eating."

"Umm, thanks," Izzie said to his back as he left the suite. She picked up the bag and quietly opened it, feeling guilty over the rule violation already. A melancholy wave washed over her, and she felt more alone here than ever. She really wished she'd asked what his name was. And that he'd come back.

4

CHAPTER FOUR

Swishing water around her mouth, Izzie tried to get rid of the chewable toothbrush taste that clung to her tongue. She spat into the sink of the library toilets and then did her best to brush out her knotted clumps of hair. The skin at the corner of her eyes was crinkled with fatigue, flushing crimson in protest. Surely, she didn't really look this bad?

The mirror just had some kind of vendetta against her.

The back seat of the car hadn't been particularly comfortable to sleep on, but at least the temperature was nice enough. It wasn't a long-term option though, she'd spent hours wondering whether someone was sneaking up to peer through the windows. Now, her eyelids twitched at the corners and even splashing her cheeks with cool water didn't seem to be reviving her. If she kept this up, she would probably miss the significance of anything she did end up finding in the records. Today she got a room.

The library had been a big distraction yesterday. Izzie only meant to have a quick look around to see if she could home in on the period she was interested in, but the bundles of papers and armfuls of leather-bound notebooks were too inviting. And too jumbled up to narrow down her focus. Nothing was arranged by time or type of document. She ached to move here for a year and sort out a working system for the entire collection.

"Hey." Izzie waved at Tessa who was in the same position as the night before, this time with a new bare-chested man on her book. "Do you have any kind of catalogue for the records? I'm really struggling to find anything."

"If there is it's probably up there in with the records," she said, keeping her place with the tip of a ruby enamelled finger while she chewed her lip. "Not sure on that one, sorry."

"But… surely there has to be a way you keep track of everything. How do you know what's there?"

"All the books are on the system, but no-one ever got around to going to through those drawers, that would take forever!"

And you're so pushed for time? Izzie bit back on her retort, she desperately needed people onside. So, she went with, "Do you think anyone else in town would know much about the history of the place? Or just where to start?"

"I'd try Sienna at The Coffee Cup, the diner over yonder, she knows everything about everything and everyone." Tessa's eyes twinkled like a proud retriever that had managed to bring over your slippers without leaving a tooth mark.

"That's actually really helpful, thanks. I'll let you get back to your book." Izzie figured the diner would be a good spot to grab some lunch later and follow up on her one lead, for now, she wanted to check something else.

Back upstairs, she dropped into the seat that the guy had sat on last night, surely, he'd know which PC was the most reliable out of these pieces of rubbish. She was prompted to set up a user account, so typed in a few details and her go-to password.

How was she supposed to describe the pool of goo she'd seen yesterday? What would make a descriptive search term? She couldn't find anything under 'Bulwark pool' or 'green goo', nothing relevant anyway. Not that the stuff *was* relevant to her goal, but she still didn't understand why she'd felt so drawn to it. Was it a side-effect of breathing it in? Her mind flickered with a lazy half-remembered thought. She'd dreamed about it. Wading into the pool that looked like it should be waist-height, yet continued to lap over her stomach, then immerse her chest, then close up over her face as she continued forward. Eyes flashed. Reminiscent of the wolf but glinting with a terrifying human intelligence.

Gasping, Izzie grabbed the corner of the desk, shaking her head to clear the overwhelming vision. She could still feel the ooze clinging to the inside of her lungs and slipping down the back of her nostrils into her throat. She needed to visit the pool again. But not yet. First, she had work to do.

5

CHAPTER FIVE

"Can I get you a cup of joe, hon?"

Izzie looked up from the menu with bleary eyes, taking in the middle-aged woman with her hair bound up and a stripy apron stretched over her ample bosom.

"If that means tea, then yes please," she croaked. After the weird incident back at the library, Izzie hadn't taken long to crash. Her muscles ached at the slightest movement and the inside of her skull felt like it had been coated with foam. She needed a proper rest. Or at least some caffeine.

"It don't, but I can rustle some up for you." The woman winked and disappeared behind the counter.

It was a sweet little place here, very typical small-town diner with the plasticky seating booths and an abundance of red, white, and blue. A handful of locals spread themselves through the place, eating lunch or catching up over a coffee. They all seemed positively friendly when talking to each other, Izzie wondered if her dishevelled appearance was more off-putting than being an out of towner.

"So, what brings you to Bulwark?" The waitress took a mug from a plastic tray and placed it on the table, the string of a tea bag dangled over the lip and swung a couple of times like a pendulum. A handful of packets of sugar and jiggers of full-fat milk were revealed from the depths of an apron pocket.

"A project," Izzie replied, looking up into a laminated tag pinned on the apron that had the name 'Sienna' printed across it. "Maybe something you could help me with?"

"Maybe if you're ordering a meal I could?" Sienna's mouth crumpled as she silently demanded an answer.

"I'll take a pancake stack, syrup and bacon please," Izzie said, handing over the menu without hesitation.

"Let me take this to the kitchen and then we'll have to look if we can't do something about your project." Sienna scribbled the order onto her notepad and headed into the back again.

Finally, a willing source! All it took was a bit of cash and she even got bacon out of it - win-win. Izzie poured in most of the little cartons of milk and stirred her tea, pulling out the tea bag once it reached the perfect colour. It didn't taste fantastic, a bit bitter for her liking, but sugar would only ruin the flavour even more. Still, it brought some normality to the situation and sharpened her focus. Hopefully, her body would be back to normal strength after eating.

"What is it you're needing to know, hon?" Sienna popped up next to her again, Izzie had no idea how the woman moved so stealthily.

She explained her situation yet again, her search for the missing part of her ancestry, the lack of a place to stop while she was here.

And Sienna just stood there and listened, hip leant against the booth as she nodded along, letting her do all the talking. Izzie was hit with desperation, she was going around in circles with these people.

"And I guess that's it," Izzie finished with a sigh. "I thought I'd be able to set myself up and dig through a few records, maybe move onto another area if I found a lead to follow. I haven't had much luck so far."

"What are you hoping to get out of this trip?" Sienna asked, head tilted as she tapped her pencil on her cheek.

"I told you, the missing part of the family tree."

"Nah, I mean why? Why you doing any of it? What are you really looking for?"

"I'm… Well, I suppose it's because it's something I've started. I put a lot of effort in and it sucks to stop now. I want to finish something I've poured my life into." Izzie took a swig of tea and slammed the cup back down, wondering where the flash of irritation came from. She wasn't going to be defeated within a matter of a couple of days.

"What happens when you're done on this project? Got something big lined up for after?" Sienna slid into the booth on the opposite bench and propped her chin on her hand, awaiting Izzie's answer.

"Not really." She sighed into her cup and rubbed her eyes. "Maybe I never even thought about finishing. It seemed like a huge thing that would take a long time, I thought I'd probably get bored before I finished. But I didn't, I just got more invested. All these people are still my family, they're interesting and vibrant and all part of me. It's like when I get the full picture I'll know where I fit into it and who I am."

"And if you don't like what you find?"

"Not everyone in the mix is a saint. There's an executioner. But there's also doctors and teachers and missionaries." They'd all given up their secrets easily like they wanted to be remembered.

"I didn't mean what you found out about other people." Sienna's knowing smile made Izzie's forehead furrow. She seemed a simple café owner yet something about her delved into the recesses of long-buried memories and dredged up the grotty pieces of Izzie's past that she'd walled over with new versions of herself every time she'd discovered something fresh about her heritage.

"So, do you know anything?"

"Not personally, but I know a man who does." Sienna's nose wrinkled, and she leant back. This invasion was over.

"Thank you so much, who should I speak to?"

"The sheriff. You said the folks you're looking for were run out of the country for witchcraft? Well, I hear that Sheriff Finnes had a run in with a witch only recent. Kidnapped his daughter. Official story is much different, of course. But I know the truth."

"That's a bit of a tenuous link to go on…" Izzie began gently, not wanting to upset her newfound ally.

"Got anything better, hon?" Sienna pursed her lips, waiting for a reply she already knew was coming.

"No."

"And here's your food, right on cue," Sienna said, slipping out of the booth. "I like you, come eat here again and tell some more about yourself, will you?"

The woman put on a beaming smile and whipped out her order pad as a pair of new customers entered The Coffee Cup.

"Oh, it's you…"

Izzie tore her gaze from the enigma that was Sienna to see the boy that had been at the library last night plonking a plate of pancakes in front of her. He wore a baseball cap with a Coffee Cup logo embroidered on the peak and a similar apron to Sienna's bound around his waist. The sweet scent of the syrup drizzled over the steaming bacon filled the air and set her salivating.

"Hey," she grinned up at him, so glad to see an almost-familiar face. Especially one that cute. "This looks incredible, thank you… Matt."

"Freaks me out when people do that," he murmured, covering his name badge with one hand.

"Okay, how about this? Hi, it's nice to see you again, I didn't catch your name last night."

"It's Matt." He handed over a knife and fork wrapped with a red napkin in a professional manner, but he lingered at the edge of her booth with his lips slightly parted, daring himself to keep talking.

"I'm Izzie," she replied, enjoying the way he was battling the twitch of a smile at the corner of his mouth.

"So, what in the world happened to you, Izzie?" He hugged the round tray he'd carried her plate over on to his chest.

"Travelled halfway across the world, nearly fell in a puddle of goo, petted a wolf, then slept in my car last night. I'm hoping the trip gets more exciting from here on."

"Err… Okay."

"Don't know anywhere that might have a room I can stay for a while, do you? I am in desperate need of a shower."

"In Bulwark? You'd be lucky. I get off at two. You can come borrow my bathroom. Wait…I don't mean like, I'm trying anything, alright? Just that you can if you want to." His fingertips turned white as his death grip on the tray intensified.

"Aww, we both know I'd kick your ass if you were. Seriously though, I'd appreciate it."

His eyebrows furrowed like he'd expected her to decline, but he nodded. "I'd better go."

"Yeah, I don't want to get you in trouble with your boss. I tried to ask her for help, but I think what actually happened was her version of an interrogation."

"Well, if there is someone with a spare room to offer you, you'll know about it soon. Don't ever tell her anything unless you want the whole town to know about it."

6

CHAPTER SIX

This lone travelling was either making Izzie bolder or stupider. Going back to a random guy's house, what was she thinking? Matt only lived a few streets away, and she drove him over there to his clipped, nervous directions. To be fair, he seemed much more intimidated of her than the other way around. He was taller and broader than her but the way he drew within himself made him seem smaller.

They pulled up at one of the smallest houses on the outskirts of town. Matt hopped out and unlocked the front door, leading her straight into a sitting room and open-plan kitchen diner. She knew it was tiny for an American house, but it still made her own flat look cramped.

The only furnishings were a deep sofa pointed towards a mid-sized TV on a unit that was slightly too small to incorporate the width of the stand and a side table with spindly legs that held up a stack of well-thumbed comic books.

The décor was sparse, the kind of simple, off-white, bland look that sellers doused their properties with so new residents could easily leave their own mark afterwards. No photos or pictures hung on the walls. At home, there was a piece of Izzie in every room; a figurine holding a teapot on the mantlepiece, scented candles in her favourite aromas along the bathroom windowsill, the epic mural in progress on the bedroom wall. Matt's sitting room could have been a low budget guest house.

He hung up his work cap on the hooks behind the door and tossed the apron into a wash basket.

"I'm guessing that's where you burned your hand?" Izzie said, slipping off her shoes and putting down the small bag filled with her toiletries and clean clothes next to them.

"Yeah. Not only do I have a dead-end job, but I'm also bad at it," he gave a self-deprecating smile and pulled open the refrigerator door.

"Don't let Sienna catch you talking like that," she warned, taking a can of pop he held out.

"She has ears everywhere, she's heard it a million times."

"It's really nice of you to do this," Izzie said, opening the can and taking a sip of pure ice and fizz. "No-one else has been much help so far."

"I'm not really doing much," he said, easing himself down into the embrace of the heavily cushioned sofa. "Shower's at the top of the stairs, my dad's away until the weekend and I only work lunchtimes so if you need anything else, I'll either be here or at the library. I'm a creature of habit."

"Thanks." Izzie picked her bag back up and trotted upstairs, pushing straight forward into the bathroom. She locked the door and heard the faint blare of the TV come on downstairs. Should she be worried? Or was he genuinely just trying to help her out? She pressed her ear to the door to try to listen for anyone coming upstairs. She held the position for a couple of minutes before she heard a chuckle from down below along with the canned laughter of whatever programme was on.

It seemed safe. Izzie felt like she was just running through the motions of how cautious a woman should be in this situation. There wasn't the pressure of panic in her chest, or a warning triggering her adrenaline. If anything, there was a calm familiarity about being here. Like if something did threaten her then Matt and Bulwark itself would step in to protect her.

I'm going crazy.

Letting her grubby clothes fall into a heap, Izzie stepped into the steaming shower and allowed the aches and toil of travel to melt off her. She washed out the grime from her hair and scrubbed every speck of her skin, wondering if she'd gather the courage to ask to come back again.

The sheriff.

He was her next target. Were you allowed to call a sheriff that? Maybe 'lead' was a better word. The talk of witches should have been absurd the second it spilt from Sienna's lips, but it linked perfectly into the small amount of information Izzie had about the family she was searching for. A woman that was the sister of her ancestor had to flee across the ocean to start a new life with her husband after her mother-in-law had been killed for the crime of witchcraft. The whole situation was barbaric and absurd, the poor woman had been burned at the stake because a group of people held onto nonsensical superstition. Though there was always the off chance that the children of the family could identify as Wiccan and still be known as witches by the people of Bulwark. Nothing would surprise her now.

For the first time since arriving, Izzie felt like she was getting somewhere. Sure, there wasn't any hard evidence yet, but she had contacts now. Bulwark had accepted her.

She had to see the goo again.

It was important. A part of a puzzle she was still gathering pieces of. The pool called to her. She had a terrible sense of direction, but she could hold out a finger and know exactly which way it was from here. She sat down suddenly, the heated water caressing her back and face while the puddle in the bottom transformed to the thick, green liquid that demanded her attention. It rose steadily, covering her thighs, then her arms as they wrapped around her slick body. Each muscle released tension she didn't know it held, she welcomed the total immersion and her hands slipped away to thump against the rough ridges of the shower mat.

Izzie breathed in and her lungs expanded with more oxygen than she'd ever inhaled before. It was like drawing in fresh air for the first time after taking a free dive. She opened her eyes and through the murk, she saw a rickety old house. A grand building that had been left in disrepair. The paint was peeling and grimy, and even the roof tiles were starting to come askew. Wooden steps led up to a closed door with a knocker that begged to be used. A decrepit mailbox caught her attention, something Lane, but before she could make out all the words, the eyes flashed across her vision like a lightning bolt searing her mind. Yellow, half animal and half human.

Choking out warm water, Izzie scraped herself up from the floor of the shower and picked her way over to the toilet. She lowered the lid and then sat on top, trembling and hugging herself. She pulled pathetically at a towel until she managed to arrange it around her dripping skin. It terrified her how unafraid she was of the vision. It had only been once she was jolted back to reality that she felt like she was drowning in the bottom of the tub.

What was wrong with her? What if it happened again, and she wasn't fit to be out alone anymore?

Just breathe.

She was fine, jetlag plus a bad night's sleep did weird things to people. There was no reason to get freaked out. There was every chance she'd half fallen asleep and had a creepy dream.

After towelling herself off, Izzie pulled on a clean, cream coloured summer dress and stood in front of the basin to brush her hair. She couldn't spot a hairdryer so had to fight with the tacky, tangled clumps to scrape them back into a ponytail.

Damn, she looked a mess. The mirror mocked her with puffy eyes and bedraggled strands escaping from her hairband. She hadn't foreseen spending any of her precious research time on going out, so didn't bother bringing any makeup or perfume. And now she was stuck in a cute guy's house looking like she'd crawled out of a sunless underwater cave. Not that she cared. She wasn't here to make an impression. Still, it would be nice to at least pretend that she was a somewhat capable human being.

After doing her best with what she had, Izzie packed up her bag and headed back downstairs. Matt was still sprawled out on the sofa, watching a stand-up comedian.

"Wow, do girls always take that long?" He grinned and stood up, walking over to where she waited at the bottom step. Her heart fluttered as he got closer and she couldn't find a single word to respond with. "I really have to get this burger grease off before I permanently smell like a fryer. Are you going to be here when I'm done?"

She could see by the way his eyes traced the length of her body that he wanted the answer to be yes. And as much as she needed to get on with going through the immense amount of information at the library, she didn't want to disappoint her one friend here.

"I could stick around for a little while," she said, leaning on the edge of the bannister and scooping back a rogue coil of hair behind her ear. "If you don't mind?"

"Sure." A smile lit his face that he tried to school, it was sweet that he was trying to play it cool. "I'd say don't steal anything but there's honestly nothing worth taking."

Izzie adored these little slips in his defence when he forgot to be nervous of her and that flicker of mischief played on his lips. She had the overwhelming urge to lay a hand on his arm as he brushed past her to ascend the stairs and couldn't fathom that she'd never touched him before. It was so right and familiar for them to share the space, Izzie's heart sank as Matt kept moving and headed up into one of the side rooms off the landing.

When she couldn't see him anymore, it was like a fog dissipating from her brain. This was not good. She didn't come this far to get distracted by a boy. How was she going to focus on the scrawl of some long-dead writer if all she was going to think about was whether Matt was thinking about her?

Four weeks, Iz, then you'll never see him again, anyway.

The thought hit her physically in the centre of her diaphragm, leaving her struggling for breath. She barely knew him. Sure, he was sweet, but Izzie had met plenty of men like that and never had this kind of connection even after knowing them for months. Ugh, it must be the accent, she'd always been a sucker for them.

She trudged over to the vacant sofa and flopped down into the cushions. The covers were thinning a little, starting to get that transparency of well-used material, but it was still cosy and supportive. The comedian continued to belt out his act down a microphone, waving his arms and encouraging the audience to bolster their applause. Izzie grabbed the remote and turned the volume down, so she could only just hear it. Then laid back into the embrace of the seat and closed her eyes. Just for a few moments.

7

CHAPTER SEVEN

"Izzie?" She heard her name from a distance, grumbled at the interruption and tucked her chin down under her arm.

"Isabelle." That caught her attention.

"No," she mumbled, forcing her eyelids up. "Not Isabelle."

"You don't like your full name?" Matt peered down at her, freshly scrubbed and dressed in a plaid shirt and jeans. He was very obviously not looking at the amount of her thigh on show where her dress had hitched up as she slept.

"No, but even if I did, it's still not that. My parents tortured me with Elizabeth, I never liked Liz or Beth either. So, I just took the Iz." She blinked and sat upright, feeling the pop of her muscles as she stretched them out from the accidental nap.

"What's wrong with it? It's a queen's name, right?"

"Yeah, that means old-fashioned and overused. Great combo."

"I like it," he said, pushing strands of fluffy, damp fringe out of his eyes.

"Then you're more than welcome to have it. Anyway, what's your plan for the rest of the day?"

"Grab some snacks and go find your long-lost great, great granny?"

"Tabitha Witham is not long lost, she's perfectly well found. Unlike a certain Bavmorda offshoot." Izzie sighed and straightened her skirt. "Wait. You're offering to help me?"

"And feed you."

This boy got more attractive by the second.

"Sienna said I should ask the sheriff some questions. There was talk of witches, admittedly. But that's what the woman they're linked to was killed for. I'm thinking they carried their traditions over here. It might be nothing, but it's all we have to go on."

Matt raised a hand as though he were attracting a teacher's attention. "Am I going to get cursed for getting involved in this?"

"Well…" Thoughts of the weird visions that afflicted her and the experiences with the goo and the wolf niggled at Izzie. "Hopefully not. But you've seen the movies, you can't do any kind of historical research without stumbling over ancient, magically protected catacombs, can you?"

"Fine. I'll take you over to Sheriff Finnes' office. At the end of his shift though, he'll be out on patrol this time of day. But if I get cursed, you find a way to break it. Deal?"

The standoffishness had melted away from Matt, replaced by an easy, goofy grin. He stood taller, the edge of his jaw beautifully cut when he wasn't buried within himself.

Confidence looks good on him.

"Of course," she said, shuffling to the edge of the broad seat so she could stand up. "I know you'd do the same for me too."

He offered her a hand and helped lift her to her feet. There was more strength there than his slender frame suggested and Izzie teetered off balance. She instinctively laid a hand on his chest to catch herself, then froze, her stomach fluttering as her thoughts wandered to what his lips would feel like.

"Even if it took forever."

Looking down at her, his voice had melted into a new softness, one that laid out each word as a legitimate promise. Izzie watched the realisation sink in that he hadn't made an offhand comment or a joke. An intense heat rippled between them, a tangible cord that looped around their waists and nudged them infinitesimally closer with each breath. She'd thought his eyes were grey, colourless. But now she could see the brighter flecks of pale green catching the sun throughout, like lightning on storm clouds.

They were still holding hands.

"Sorry," he said, loosening his grip, teasing out the last second of contact. "I was just…"

"About to feed me?" Izzie giggled, folding her arms, worried her hands would unconsciously seek the buttons of his shirt. 'Feed?' What an idiot, why didn't she say 'kiss?'

Because she wasn't brave enough for that.

Not yet.

8

CHAPTER EIGHT

After sharing an obnoxiously large pizza and watching an old superhero movie, it was time to go and meet the sheriff. Izzie pulled her rental car out from the driveway and let Matt direct her from the passenger seat in between his badly sung renditions of whatever country rock songs popped up on the radio.

This must be it. A reversal of fortunes. Surely the sheriff would have something useful to add to the investigation. If she had this thing wrapped up within a few days, she certainly wouldn't mind spending the rest of her trip here in Bulwark. Not if it involved more days like this.

As the police station came into view, Izzie slowed the car and her hand drifted down to the centre console. Her fingertips brushed the gentle warmth of skin instead of the firm plastic she'd been anticipating. A deep, purposeful thrum vibrated through her chest like her heart was beating fully for the first time. Every inch of her body fluttered with anticipation as though there was more danger in that one touch than when she'd come face to face with the wolf.

"Oh, you want me to shut up?" Matt asked.

"No. I'm just not used to driving an automatic," Izzie replied with a laugh, fighting the urge to trail her fingers over more of his arm. "I was trying to shift down."

"Maybe you need another note?" He teased, tapping her 'Keep On The Right!!!!' sticker. It was impossible to watch the road when the curves of his shoulder and back occupied the corner of her vision as he leaned across so closely.

"Well, if you came to England, you'd need a whole essay attached to your steering wheel." Izzie took a steadying breath as she pulled up outside the station and switched off the engine.

"I'd make you drive," he said with a grin, then climbed out.

If he made that effort and came all that way to see her, she'd gladly chauffeur him around the entire country. Not that she should be thinking like that. Izzie had never liked the thought of a long-distance relationship and the idea that she was even considering it with someone she barely knew was crazier than anything else that had happened here so far.

The family tree mural had been something that she'd worked on for a few years now, and it used to be the most exciting thing in her life. Here she was on the cusp of finding that elusive final piece of the story, yet it barely seemed important now. She needed to get her head in the game to make sure she got everything she needed from the sheriff.

Matt led the way into the building and had a quick conversation with the first officer they bumped into. He headed off into the back, then returned a few moments later with good news.

"Sheriff Finnes will see you, just head on through. You know the way." The officer smiled and gave Matt a wink, waving them on their way.

"And you seem like such a sweet, law-abiding citizen," Izzie said with a mock gasp.

"Err, I kinda experimented with spray paint for a while a few years back. Purely for artistic expression, of course."

"True artists are never appreciated in their own time," she whispered as she followed him into the office.

Sheriff Finnes wore authority as easily as Izzie would throw on a jacket. Even sat on a metal chair with his hands clasped over the bundles of files on his desk, his height and bulk made Matt look like a scrawny child.

Something pulsed within Izzie's mind, a fight-or-flight response screaming along her veins. She flickered a look towards Matt, searching for reassurance that he hadn't brought her here for this man to kill her.

He was back to his reticent self, hands in pockets and not quite meeting the sheriff's hard gaze.

"What can I do for you, Matthew? Everything okay with your dad?" Sheriff

Finnes' voice echoed around the room, owning the space and pushing Izzie further within herself. Her pulse fluttered in a completely different way than before. She poised on the balls of her feet, controlled her ragged breath.

"Yes, sir," Matt said, "I brought my friend over, Izzie, she's here for a few weeks working on a project and just had a few questions that Sienna thought you might be able to help her with."

"That right, Izzie?" The sheriff's deep brown eyes bored through to her soul and she swore she saw a flicker of recognition. What was going on in this town?

"Yes... sir."

"Call me Clay. You're a visitor here, right? So, you won't be making the kind of trouble that means you should call me 'sir.' Tell me what's going on and how I can help you, Izzie."

She slowly laid out her story but didn't dare give any details. She left out the wolf and the goo, couldn't bring herself to tell him any of the meagre facts she'd found so far. There was something seriously wrong here.

"Sounds like you've come a long way for this," Clay rubbed his chin and scrunched his face up for a second, mulling over her words. "This family of yours got a name?"

Izzie's throat ran dry, her lips frozen in place.

"Bavmorda?" Matt sounded out the unfamiliar syllables. "That's right, isn't it?"

Izzie felt her head nod gently and gripped the folds of her dress to stop her hands shaking. Clay's eyes narrowed, his lip twitched. The sheriff reached down, unclipped a gun from his side, and laid it on the table with the barrel aimed directly at Izzie's stomach. She searched the man's face for any sign of what his intentions were. The fact that he could carry around a live weapon, possibly use it, flummoxed her. She could get shot here today and then it would only be their word against a sheriff if they wanted to try to seek justice.

"I've probably policed this town longer than you've been alive, I can tell you there's no way you'll find anything relating to a family by that name." Clay tapped a finger on his sidearm and stared at her face. "How long did you say you're in the country for?"

"Three more weeks after this one." Izzie was captured by the dark mouth of the gun barrel, she wished she knew how to tell if the safety was on from where she stood.

"I'll be checking you don't overstay your travel authorisation," Clay said, "Don't give me a reason to come find you."

Matt shared a wide-eyed look with her and shrugged his shoulders. Another dead-end.

"If I see you anywhere near my home, you'll be spending the rest of this little holiday in my cells, do you understand?" Clay stood to his full height, shoving back his chair with a metallic screech, and laid his palm on the gun. "And if you so much as look at my daughter, I'll be shooting first and asking questions later."

"Go," Matt murmured into her ear, scooping Izzie out of the door and striding down the corridor. He bundled her along in his arms all the way out of the station until they stepped out into the dying warmth of the evening.

She could feel the greyness in her face, knew her eyebrows were stretched up into slim arcs somewhere in her hairline. Her lungs tripped over as she tried to slow the hyperventilation and compose herself.

"It's okay," Matt said, pulling her in close so she could rest her forehead on his shoulder, "His daughter was kidnapped a bit over a year ago. They got her back recently, but it looks like it hit him harder than I thought. I wouldn't have brought you here if I knew he'd flip like that, I'm sorry."

"He threatened to shoot me…" Saying it out loud made Izzie's eyes prickle with tears and she clung onto him, an uncontrollable tremor taking over her body.

"You're fine," he said, tightening his arms around her to still her shivering, "Let's get you home."

"I don't have…"

"Come on." His lips were against the top of her head, the warmth of his breath in her hair. "I'm not leaving you anywhere like this."

9

CHAPTER NINE

"I feel like such an idiot." The cool glass pressed into Izzie's temple, the thrum of her elevated heart rate pulsing against her skull.

"He's not usually like that." Matt was in the driver's seat, backing out of the parking space and glancing over at the door of the station. "Sheriff Finnes was always a decent guy, treated people fairly and made sure the town was safe. Even while Claire was missing.

I don't have a clue what got into him just then but it's not right."

"No, it's not." Izzie twirled a piece of her hair around a finger, using the pointless, repetitive task to ignore the dose of shock trickling around her system.

"Do you think he was right? About not finding anything about the Bavmordas?" Matt asked, laying a reassuring hand on her forearm.

"I don't know. I don't know how he could be so sure unless he did know something? I don't know how to find out or what I'm going to do next either…" she trailed off, closing her eyes and groaning, taking in a trickle of the strength lent to her through his touch.

"If you want me to go talk to him alone, I will," Matt said, turning down the blast of guitar-fuelled music on the radio. "He's always been straight with me; cut me some slack when I needed it, kicked my butt when I deserved it."

"No. You've done more than enough," Izzie replied. "I don't want to put you in that situation. I'll figure something out. I just need to come up with a new plan, I need to go through my notes and see what I'm missing.

There has to be something I haven't considered."

"Iz, you're freaked out, exhausted, and jet-lagged. How about you take the night off and come back with fresh eyes tomorrow? I'll put you up, we'll even stop at the store and get you some tea if it'll make you feel better?"

"Tea always makes me feel better."

By the time they got back to Matt's house with a bagful of groceries, Izzie had calmed down enough to start thinking properly. Her temples still throbbed with the overwhelming stress of meeting Clay Finnes, she'd known he was bad news the second she'd stepped into his office. She wasn't intending on making the mistake of crossing his path again. What was that jerk's problem? It wasn't like *she'd* kidnapped his daughter.

Matt made her some tea, she took him back through to the kitchen to show him how to do it properly, then they sprawled out on the sofa with some mindless comedy reruns on in the background.

"I'm not getting in the way of anything you planned tonight, am I?" Izzie took a sip of tea and savoured the wonderful scorch down her throat.

"I was trying to think of a way to wind Tessa up on my way into the library but that can wait until tomorrow."

"You spend a lot of time there, huh?"

"Yeah, I don't have a computer here. I like checking out the web comics and design tutorials. I guess I'd like to do something like that myself one day." Matt scratched the back of his neck and looked over to the TV screen, not at it but through it.

"You should," Izzie said. "Seriously, there's nothing stopping you. It's like calligraphy, it just takes some practice."

"Well… It's that… that the rest of the time I kinda have a project of my own."

He scrubbed at his eyes with the heels of his hands then chewed his lip while she waited for him to continue.

"My mom."

"What about her?" Izzie ventured, laying aside her almost-empty mug.

"Anything. My dad never told me about her, whether she left or… or if she died. There're no photos, no memories. I've tried looking up my dad's past, and there's no point searching for other Browns, it's the most common surname in the universe."

"That's awful, for him to keep that from you. I do have some experience with genealogy research if you need a hand though?" Her heart swelled to think that she might be able to pay back a little of the kindness she'd received.

"That would be amazing. But only if you've got time, I don't want you to waste the few weeks you're over here when you've got your own to stuff to figure out."

"If it were for you, it wouldn't be a waste," she said, catching the little upturn at the corner of his mouth. "If I don't find anything out while I'm here I could always email you? Or call you?"

She handed over her phone with the new contact option open and gave her best hopeful smile. Either she was about to get shot down or tied up in something that was going to get agonisingly painful at some point. But sat here, getting to bask in his calm presence, it was worth it.

"Text me yours," he said, handing her phone back after tapping in a number.

She saved his details and typed out a new message.

"LadyMurray? That's one pretentious email address." He gave her a side glance with a raised eyebrow.

"Well, I am descended from royalty. I made that account the day I found my royal connection. Of course, pretty much everyone fits into the lineage somehow, but I won't let that get in the way of boasting."

"I've never seen anyone boast through an email address before. If you believe mine it makes me a cartoon ninja with a magic sword."

Izzie had an inkling, or at least hoped, that he'd only worn a shirt today to look nice for her. She wondered how much of his wardrobe was more like the dorky anime top he'd had on yesterday. And she ached with the urge to dig down to uncover every real part of Matt.

"Will you put on some of the shows you like? I didn't recognise the character you were wearing when I first met you."

"Izzie, are you trying to seduce me?" He tilted his head on one side, he thought she thought he was joking but she could read the telltale glimmer of hope in the way he fixated on her mouth.

"Not yet," she licked her lips and leaned forward slightly, "But if you don't pick up on my very obvious signals soon, I will have to start."

His look broke her. Like they'd been aching for the moment for a thousand years and finally, desperately, they'd given in. The softness of his lips coupled with the hunger and passion in his kiss brought a soft moan to her throat and curled her toes. He reached over to draw her closer, his other hand cupping her cheek. She could never want anyone else ever again.

In a tangle of limbs, Izzie pulled Matt down on top of her, his weight pushing her into the wide cushions of the sofa. She wrapped her legs around him and he pressed down into her, the firm thrust of his hips made her gasp, but he stifled her with his tongue. He kissed her for either an eternity or an instant, either way it wasn't enough. They moved rhythmically together, fully clothed, yet somehow Izzie felt more exposed and fulfilled than she ever had. Her fingers traced the smooth skin where his shirt had rucked up, fascinated by this tiny new piece of his body. He teased down the scoop neck of her dress so he could explore the smooth curve of her breasts, kneading and sucking her into submission.

She needed more.

Izzie tugged at the hem of his shirt and Matt tore it off. She chewed her lip, breath catching as she roved his bare chest and the trail of hair beneath his belly button. He paused for a second, eyes glittering at her love-drunk expression, then he tossed the shirt aside, knocking over the teacup with a clatter and splashing the carpet.

"Ignore it," he panted, lips already seeking hers as she gripped his belt and directed him back against her.

She shifted her hands and began to unbuckle it.

"Are you sure?" He whispered. She could feel how much he wanted this, how he'd barely stopped himself for long enough to voice those few ragged words.

"I've never been surer about anything."

He slid his hands up her skirts and along the contour of her bottom. His roving fingers found her underwear, she lifted her hips into him so he could slip them off. It was nearly impossible to ignore the gentle caress between her thighs long enough to concentrate on unhooking his belt, but finally, she wrestled the button open and released him.

After this, she could never let him go.

10

CHAPTER TEN

"Hmm?" Izzie mumbled, tugging the covers up around her chin.

"Go back to sleep," Matt said, planting a quick kiss on her forehead, "You need it."

"So do you."

They'd stayed up all night talking. Well, half the night talking and half getting to know each other in other ways…

"I have to go to work, or Sienna will destroy me. Her words last time I was late."

"I miss you," Izzie said. "Will you stay if I show you my boobs?"

"Yes, so don't." He covered his eyes, peeking through his middle fingers. "I'll be done at two. There's a spare key on the hook if you want to go out, just let me know where to meet you."

He kissed her again, this time on the lips, lingering an extra second. Then he checked the time on his phone, swore, and bolted downstairs.

How could something be both the best and the most unfair thing that had ever happened to her? Why here, why now? Why couldn't he at least live on the same continent as her?

Izzie sighed and plumped the pillow that was covered in Matt's smell. If she was pining already, how was she going to survive going back to England and not seeing him for months at a time? The realisation that she was already on a countdown to leave smacked into her like a physical pain. She battled back the wave of tears that threatened to spill out. She needed to enjoy this time while she could. Afterwards would come after.

Matt met her at the library after work. Izzie had already spent a few hours there, trawling through the never-ending wads of paperwork and slim volumes of records from Bulwark's history. When population reports were crammed in directly behind crumbling, musty newspapers from a completely different decade, Izzie had to take a break to stop herself from marching downstairs to strangle Tessa.

"Hey," Matt said as he entered, hooking her by the waist and pulling her against his body for a kiss. "Find anything yet?"

"Only one gorgeous guy."

She didn't think he'd ever let her go, his arms holding her firmly to his chest as he nuzzled her ear.

"So, are you sure you even like England?" He murmured.

"I think you need to come and see it, then you'll realise that you don't want to come back here." She laid a hand on his chest, feeling the steady increase in his pulse when she moulded herself into him and tilted her chin up, seeking his lips.

"Am I invited?" He asked, teasing her by gently brushing his bottom lip to hers.

"I don't do holiday flings," she replied, trying to capture him as he kept just out of reach, "If you don't come, you'll be giving me a bad reputation."

"Well, I'll have to make sure that doesn't happen."

Just as Izzie thought she couldn't bear his teasing any more, he pressed his mouth to hers. So agonisingly slowly. The tender caress was almost worse than not touching him at all, the hot pouring of desire took over her senses until all she could feel was their connection, not just physically but as though even their souls were entwined and could never be separated.

"We need to get some research done," Matt said, "Before there's a public indecency incident. But I'm definitely picking this back up when we get home."

When we get home. That melted her. Maybe one day that would mean something else, more than a temporary lodging on a visit. It felt so tangible already, waking up to see him pushing the dark fringe from his face and reaching over to stroke her cheek. Why was their every interaction, each touch and conversation, as though it were part of a well-loved and perfectly co-ordinated routine? Last night she found that he knew every way to make her feel comfortable, to make her forget that she was conscious of the little pudgy roll on her stomach or the birthmark that covered the left corner of her ribcage. And she automatically knew the words to encourage him that cracked any last vestiges of the shell he hid behind.

Was this love? Or magic?

He slowly released her, rubbing his thumb over the back of her hand, then dropped into the chair at his PC, putting his feet up on the next one. Izzie stood behind him and watched him open up his account.

"So, what have you got so far?" He asked.

Izzie opened the images on her phone, taking him through the stages of her research.

"See, here's my direct line, it goes back this way until it gets to this bit, that's where the Bavmorda's records disappear. You can't get much from just this, maybe the closer relatives names but I've done checks on all of them. One weird thing you might see is that there are hardly any girls in my line. I was the first one born since this break off that I'm researching."

"Oh, you're Elizabeth on there?" Matt pinched to zoom in on her place in the mural then looked up with a glint of mischief in his eyes.

"Well, I didn't want to confuse anyone in the future if they see it. Plus, I like how the capital 'E's come out in this calligraphy style."

"So, what goes here?" Matt pointed to a clear space at the side of her name and raised his eyebrows.

"Yeah, we'll see, stud. You need to prove your virility first."

"I don't think I have much left to prove." He shrugged and turned back to the PC and pondered over the search bar.

"I've done a million searches," she said, but it was probably several million, really.

"Maybe there's something about the town I know that you don't? Like buildings or other old families from around here you haven't heard about?" His fingers flew across the keyboard as he typed out different names and skimmed the results, intent on finding an answer.

Izzie let her hand trail his shoulder one last time as she wandered back over to the mess of drawers and heaved the next wad out with a frustrated sigh. More newspapers from the wrong era, some letters that had been addressed to a very minor local celebrity, there was even an old receipt for a tuna sandwich in here! This was going to be agonising and pointless. Maybe she should just forget this whole ridiculous venture? The drawers lined up around the edge of the room, dozens of them, all shuffled up. Even if there was a scrap of information she could use, there were no guarantees of her digging it out before the end of her trip.

No. She wasn't the kind of person that just gave up. So what if she didn't get through everything before she went? It wasn't like she didn't have any reason to come back.

She watched Matt with his intent eyes on the screen, scrolling the mouse wheel while his pupils flickered over the information. He leaned forward, elbows on the desk. His mouth dropped into a perfect 'O' and he scrolled faster.

Izzie pelted across the room before he could tell her that he had something. How had he got a lead already?

"Look!" He jabbed a finger at the post, underlining the name 'Bavmorda' with his neatly trimmed fingernail.

"What on Earth did you find, Matt?" Izzie gasped. "How did you get this?"

"It's new. See, the time stamp is a couple of hours ago. It's a kid named Jacob. It's pretty crazy, so don't get your hopes up, but it might be something."

"Nothing is crazier than Tessa's 'filing system,' go ahead."

"Jacob says that he came through Bulwark with his parents and his sister not long ago. Apparently, a witch named Bavmorda captured him, his sister, and some other kids. She wanted their blood to stay youthful."

"Matt, come on." Izzie folded her arms and stepped back from the desk. She'd really believed he'd found something.

"Yeah, it's dumb, but listen to this. His parent's car crashed into a puddle of what could be a kind of toxic slime and his mum died, he's putting this out there to tell the world what 'really happened' to his mum. We have that puddle, Iz, and a visitor really did die in the hospital from that crash. I think he might be who he says he is. And he says that the Bavmorda house is along the road at the other side of the slime, on a 'Linden Lane.' Witch crap aside, it looks like a solid lead."

She didn't dare tell him. Mention the pull that goo had over her or the way it permeated her dreams. Linden Lane? Wasn't that what was written on the post box in her vision? It should have been obvious. The link between the pool and her bloodline, her body had somehow known what her mind had refused to acknowledge.

"I've seen it. That slimy stuff, I should have known…" Izzie found herself murmuring.

"Why?"

"It's just…" A moment ago, she didn't think she'd ever keep anything from Matt, but now it sounded crazy and like she was buying into Jacob's fantasies. She didn't want him to think she was insane. "That road is the only place in town I didn't check out. Makes sense that the answers would be there."

"Always the last place you look," he said with a grin, shutting the PC down. "Let's go."

11

CHAPTER ELEVEN

The pit of Izzie's stomach gnawed with anxiety. She couldn't think of a reason for Matt not to come with her, yet she didn't want him seeing her freak out over the goo. Didn't want to see the revulsion in his eyes when she leaned out to it like it was a beloved pet. No, not a pet, a guard dog that kept her safer than he ever could.

She changed direction.

"It's that way," Matt said, pointing back to the last turning.

"I'm dropping you off at home," she replied.

"What's up?"

"This is a thing I've been working on forever. And don't think I don't appreciate your help, I wouldn't be anywhere without it. I just want to say that it was me that found whatever's there when I get there, you know? It's kind of my big quest and the end of my journey. I need to do it on my own. Do you get that?"

"I get it, Iz, honestly, but it's out of town and dangerous, people have said there are wolves coming back to the area. Don't forget there were actual kidnappings not that long ago." His voice bled with worry, and she chose to ignore his hand on her wrist.

"I promise I'll be safe," she said, staying the course, "I've been near there before, and I was fine. If there's any sign of danger, I'll get out of there straight away and come back for you. I need this, Matt, please."

He grunted and withdrew his touch to fold his arms. She had her way. This was for the best. They'd be so much better off once she traced the Bavmordas and reached her goal. Then she could spend the rest of her time focused on him, without having to worry about the influence of the goo while he was around.

"Just so you know, I am not happy about this." Matt climbed out of the passenger seat and leant his arm on the roof as he spoke to her.

"I'll be straight back to celebrate," Izzie promised. "This is it, I can feel it. Then you get one hundred percent of my attention for the next few weeks."

"I could be happy about that, I suppose. But stay safe, Iz. I'd feel really guilty if you went and got mauled by wolves, or kidnapped, or cursed."

"Yeah, but you'd come rescue me, right?"

"Even if it took forever." The door closed with a clunk and Matt stepped away, his thunderstorm eyes on her until she pulled out of their driveway.

12

CHAPTER TWELVE

She knew the way. The draw of the goo had taken a background while she'd been so intensely immersed in passion, but it had always been there. A knot tied around the centre of her core that wound her in like a fish on a hook. She didn't want to wriggle or fight; she wanted to meet the fisherman.

Izzie parked in the same spot as before, not wanting to intrude upon the peace of the pool. When others mentioned it, they called it toxic or vile. How couldn't they see the truth? That it was purer and more wonderful than the paintings of fairy ponds, that it held life and blossomed with prosperity and sustenance.

This time she remembered walking there. The trees lining her path. The smooth trickle of the wind making music in their branches. She longed to draw them, to trace their winding connections on her reams of paper and let her calligraphy pens dance with their unique patterns. The shapes were words, told their own story, branched off into new directions like the history she sought.

Here. The liquid spread before her, diminished from her last visit like it was struggling to survive. Izzie wept. Let her tears mingle with the pool and feed her own essence into it. It needed her. She needed it.

The liquid coated her fingers like a layer of paint as she dipped them in up to the middle knuckles. When she drew them out, it glittered on her skin like crushed gemstones mixed with oil. She traced a rune on each cheek, another on her forehead. Their forms and meanings twined from her instincts.

"That is not for you," a feminine voice reached Izzie's ears, stopped her heart.

"It is," she replied, searching the clearing for the source. "It's been calling me."

"No. I have." A layer of wispy mist gathered over the pool, coalescing into the figure of a shapely woman just in front of the crashed car.

"Who are you?" Izzie wasn't afraid, didn't question the impossibility of what unfolded, she reached down again for the goo.

A spark jolted from the wisp, knocking her hand away.

"I told you that wasn't yours," the voice crackled like a bad signal, the wisp flickering in and out of sight. "And I am the one you've been searching for. I am Bavmorda."

"The Bavmordas were a family, what do you know about them?" The runes were drying to a crust on her face, leeching a cool throb deep into her skin.

"I am their culmination. They were so weak. Pointless existences. Even my own daughter was a failure, now dead. As she should be. Fortunately, I am not so easy to kill. She was my deepest regret and the source of my shame. But you, Elizabeth, you are different. You must feel that power. The knowledge of ages, the thirst for more, the ability to take whatever you desire. You want that, don't you? Sheriff Finnes saw that in you." Bavmoda's voice caressed Izzie's soul, and she sat in the slick mud, disregarding the filth ruining her clothes as she felt her eyelids droop to half-closed. Docile.

The wisp drifted over until the crackly, static edges tickled her arms and made her hairs stand up. Izzie watched them with fascination, a little row of slender soldiers standing to attention. The mist surrounded her, blurring her vision, worming its way into her nostrils until she choked on the cloying air. Her lungs burned, her cheeks ripped open with agony along the runes. Her forehead smoked, pulsing power into her muscles and she *pushed*.

The mist tore from her insides, leaving her windpipe raw. Izzie coughed and heaved in breaths from her hands and knees. She touched her face, expecting blood on her fingertips but only finding the ash of scorched goo.

"How?" Bavmorda shrieked, taking her busty form again. "You should be ignorant; innocent and ripe."

"Well, maybe I am ignorant, but I'm sure not innocent." Izzie dragged herself to her feet, her limbs heavy with fatigue.

"If only you knew. You'd be magnificent, maybe the strongest of all. If the sheriff and his friends hadn't destroyed my body, I would have taken you under my wing, made you my daughter and given you the world for all eternity. We would have drunk blood, seduced men, claimed all the youth and strength we desired. But you have something I need. My only female relative alive today. Your form isn't perfect, but I can change that once I own it. A slimmer waist, perkier breasts. You've wasted a lot of what you've inherited. But I can work with it."

Izzie's rage at the wisp's cruel remarks stung, and she gathered it close. When Bavmorda dispersed and surged at her again, Izzie released. The surrounding air buzzed with flickers of her scorching anger. How dare this thing try to use her?

The wisp spun to avoid Izzie's power, drenched itself in the pool, then swam through the darkening air in a galaxy of glinting specks. It smashed Izzie to the floor, pinning her into the slop and forcing its way into her nose and mouth and ears. She writhed against the mass, searching for the anger again, it was slipping away as panic overthrew her senses. The power was there, somewhere. It was an inheritance, it was in her blood. But so was Bavmorda, she was coursing through Izzie's veins, taking hold and laying claim to every cell of her body.

Everything she was begun slipping away. Izzie couldn't remember her parent's faces anymore. A man wearing an old-fashioned military uniform popped up instead. Didn't she have a brother? Or was it a sister she saw as they ran through dingy, dirt-encrusted streets, hiking up their dresses? Matt. Was he still there? She thought his eyes were supposed to look like flashes of lightning, but they were dark now, such a deep brown they could be black.

Bavmorda's memories pushed Izzie out, overwriting her. These people were Bavmorda's family. Her father, her sister, her husband. But weren't some of them Izzie's family too? She finally put a face to Nancy Smith, she knew her. The woman whose sister had emigrated to America, fleeing the executioner's torch when her mother-in-law had wrongly been charged with witchcraft. No, that was tangled up in their line. The gift that flowed through their blood and manifested in the female descendants.

She saw more, finally gained those branches that were missing from the mural. The people closest to Bavmorda. She'd betrayed each one. Cared only for beauty and magic. Cast aside her own daughter. Izzie reached to their memories, used the dying sparks of the remnants of her soul to tell them.

I know you. I remember you.

She told them all. Each individual that made up the possibility of her birth or also extended from that root. She told them that she knew their job, who they'd married, where they'd lived. More of her memory fled with each second but still, she persevered.

'Mary, you did so much good for charity, thank you.'

'Lisa, to provide for your children, you worked three jobs after your husband died. I swear I used to know his name, but she's taken it from me. I'm sorry.'

'Nancy, you sparked my passion to find this place, I wouldn't have met Matt if it weren't for you.'

'Izzie,' their voices thrummed together as one, *'You remember us, we remember you.'*

Flash after flash burst across Izzie's mind. Faces and dates and facts and sensations returned to her, each one elbowing a piece of Bavmorda from where she squatted in her body. She remembered. Her parents' stern warnings as she left for her solo trip. Her brother calling her a dork yet being the only one that put up with her rambling about their shared history. Except for Matt, and he was there too. His little goofy grin when she flirted with him, the pattern of raised specks on the back of his hand where he'd splashed himself with oil at work, the exquisite sensation of his skin sliding against her own.

She knew who she was. She was Elizabeth Murray, and she was not going to lay back and let a creepy old witch steal her body.

A wail hissed from the cloudy entity, it leaked from her nose as Izzie opened her eyes. The grotesque mud clung to her back and her hair as she forced herself into a seating position and reached her hand desperately for the puddle of goo. It would protect her, enhancing her ability to defend herself.

"Wait!" Bavmorda shrieked, flowing into a more transparent version of her figure. She pointed to the tree line.

"No…" Izzie's voice broke, and she jerked her hands away from the goo, holding them up where her torturer could see them.

She could see Matt from the corner of her eye, his gaze vacant and one arm slumped at his side. The other held a carving knife to his own throat, edge pressed so tightly to his flesh that it could split at any second.

"I don't want him. All the power of our bloodline to take the heart and body of any man you desire, and this is what you choose?" Bavmorda said, the essence of a sneer flickering on her insubstantial face. "I'll let him go if you give me what I want."

"You'll kill again though…"

"You honestly think you're strong enough to defeat me? With no training, no experience, and the body of your lover convulsing in a pool of his own blood within eyesight? I'll kill again either way. But this way, I won't kill him."

"He wouldn't be able to forgive himself…"

"He won't remember a thing, no-one will."

"I want him to remember," Izzie whispered. "Promise me that."

"Save his life and curse him with a single act? You truly are one of us, Elizabeth…"

EPILOGUE

"I just don't know what to do, Doc." Jerry Brown pushed back the thick locks from his forehead and sighed into his cupped hands. He peered through the window on the door to see the back of his son's head, tipped down into his chest. "He's always been a weird kid, but since he called me that night…"

"And you're sure he's wrong?"

"Doc, he said a witch pulled his girlfriend into that sludge. I never heard a thing about this girl before. The sheriff had that pool dredged and came up with nothing. He's hysterical, poor boy can barely breathe since. And he's got a slit on his neck; not deep, not bloodied, but you can see why I'm freaking out." Jerry clamped his hands together and tried to stop the tremor jerking through his leg.

"He could've seen her fall in, maybe he thought she drowned in there, but she came out after he'd gone, and a wolf got her? Or she went back to wherever she came from." Doc laid a conciliatory hand on Jerry's shoulder, but he shrugged it off.

"You don't get it. Matt's been telling me that people in town met this girl. Tessa, Sienna, even Clay. Everyone I talked to don't know nothing about her. Never seen her, didn't even know a foreign girl was in town. But he's flipped out, doc. Swears she's real, crying for her and going back to that damn place. Just keeps saying he has to try, even if it takes forever. He don't know where her car went though, don't have a single thing to prove it. But I know grief, Doc. And everything about what he's going through convinces me that he just lost a girl he was in love with."

"Jerry. This is tough for you, I know. But we both know that he's had… episodes before. Maybe it's worth you getting a professional to speak to him?"

"I know, I know, Doc. But something just… it feels different this time."

"There's one other possible cause."

"Doc…" Jerry tried to make his voice a warning.

"No, Jerry. I really think it's about time you talked to Matt about his mother."

Other books by Kay MacLeod

The Constellation Saga

Heirs of Power

The Mage-Lord's Legacy

For more on my books or to get in touch with me –

Visit my website- kaymacleodbooks.com

Like my Facebook page- facebook.com/KayMacLeodFantasy

Follow me on Twitter- twitter.com/KayMacLeodBooks

Follow me on Instagram-
instagram.com/kaymacleodbooks/

Follow me on Pinterest-
pinterest.co.uk/KayMacLeodBooks/

Huge thanks to cover designer R.L. Jackson

authorrljackson.com/

Read on for the first chapter from The Body, Volume Six of The Bulwark Anthology…

Check out the next book in the Bulwark Anthology:

The Body

Kate Kelley

1

CHAPTER ONE

It's cold, but I don't care. I don't feel it, not really, the sharp wind tearing at the edges of my free-bleeding lashes, the cuts on my cheekbones. My feet march out a path only they know through the shallow snow-turned sludge, the destination irrelevant; just *far away, far away, far away.*

Vic gave me a good fight tonight, the kind that made me second-guess myself, the kind that made me hurt, like really hurt, in a way I hadn't in a long time. But that was Vic--he'd been hurting me since he'd showed up in the club a year ago. We matched in almost every way physically--both middleweight, both 6'. That's fine, I revel in the fight, and the rest of the boys haven't been a challenge for me in a long while. But tonight, I was supposed to win. I had the rage on my side, and I didn't use it. It was so bottled up and today, it shot out like a shook-up soda bottle. I let it, I let the rage consume me, the memories of my tiny sister, dead on the floor, my mother standing over her. It was her anniversary today, little Josie's been dead for eighteen years, and I was supposed to be fighting for her. I couldn't fight my mom, she's dead too--electric chair, back when they did that kind of thing. I let the fight slip, I let the rage slip out, too frantic, too chaotic, and I couldn't control it anymore. I lost it in that cage today, and I fucking dropped the ball.

My fist shoots out, connecting with the tree closest to me. The bark cracks and I let my fist fall, the already-bruised knuckles numb and vibrating from the hit. I shake my hand out, wincing, and inspect my bark-encrusted cuts. I forgot what it felt like to punch without gloves.

I come out here after my losses, out here in the forest, to breathe and just take a step back out in the open. To feel normal--human--again, instead of a performer in a cage. To reclaim my body as my own before going back to the fight. I'd win next week. I was just messed up from the memories; I just needed to clear them out of my head.

I start jogging, weaving in and out of the trees, going further into the thick wooded area than I normally would go. But the wind stops chasing me, with the trees blocking me, and my boots get steadier on the uneven terrain. With each boot thud, my past springs up to torture me.

Thud. Josie's bloodied, small face staring up at me.

Thud. Mom convulsing in the chair, her eyes wide on me.

Thud. Every kid's face I beat while on the streets.

Thud. Smashing in Vic's face in the cage. Watching him smile up at me as his arm lifts in victory.

Splash.

I stop, holding on to the trunk of a tree next to me, and look down as my chest heaves with gulping oxygen.

"What the fuck…" I've run right into some sort of marsh; my boots drowned up to the ankles. It's hard to see the consistency of the marsh, as the dull, gray November afternoon is quickly turning to evening, and the trees shroud most of sunlight that might be there. I bend over slightly to peer at it more closely, moving my head to catch a shred of light. Green. It's green, like the green of algae. I stand back up with a frown, noting how far the pond scum or whatever it was seems to go. I can't see the end of it. A swamp of some sort, I decide, and take a sniff. Doesn't smell like swamp, though. No sulfur, no rotting egg smell…

It's getting really dark now, and a blast of chilly air blasts up my t-shirt, despite the fact that the wind has been still for the past half hour.

I turn, ignoring the strange feeling that is prickling over my skin now while I make my way back. I turn, and turn, but realize soon that I have no idea how I have gotten here, and that the woods are far thicker than I anticipated.

Another chill sweeps up my spine, and the forest grows darker.

"Whatever," I mumble, "I've gotten out of worse."

And it wasn't like I was dying to get back to my tiny flat, anyway, besides the promise of a tepid shower and shelter from the cold. But I could build a fire. In soggy, November swampy woods, though, Rudd? Really?

I growl at my inner doubts and stomp on.

That's when I hear it. The barest echo of a song bouncing through the bodies of the trees. *"...just a poor boy though my story seldom told..."*

It is like the purest, sweetest voice I'd ever heard, and my heart seizes up. I turn in every direction, trying to find the source of the singer.

When I find nothing but gray shadows, I shake my head hard and continue on. I need sleep. *Now.*

"..seeking out the poorer quarters where the ragged people go..."

I swivel abruptly with a growl. "Show yourself," I shout. I am out my mind. A sweet woman singing in the dark, deep wood in the middle of an unusually chilly November night, especially for Georgia. And upon the second verse of the song, it was clear it wasn't a girl singing, but a woman.

I am insane. Maybe I should visit the doctor, maybe I could start seeing a therapist--

"Wait," a shaking voice pleads near my right ear.

I swivel, my fists clenched to keep from pummeling the speaker, and stop. Actually, everything stops. My blood, my heart, my brain. The whole fucking planet stops spinning.

After what could be a full five minutes, I somehow push the words up and out of my throat. "You…you aren't real."

"You see me."

I back up another step when I feel her come closer. And I *can* feel her--it's sort of a soft heat, like lazy summer rays on my skin.

There isn't much I'm scared of, that I would run away from. I'd pretty much scrubbed away any fear left in my body when I'd run away from foster care and lived on the streets as a kid. But this--this was something else. This was some honest-to-God fucked-up shit.

"You're not real," I whisper, disgusted at how scared I sound.

Her body--if you could call it that, moves forward, then, as if sensing my imminent retreat, backs up. She puts her arms up, palms out, as if in surrender. "I just want to talk," she pleads, again in that low, desperate voice. Her voice sounds more solid now.

Her body glows--like--like a fucking blue lava lamp, but softer, so that you aren't quite sure unless you stare hard. And her body is see-through. Transparent. I can see the tree behind her that she stands in front of. Beyond that, I can't focus on her. It's like she can't quite come into focus--her features blur like static on a busted tv.

"Am I drugged?" The words rasp out of me like sandpaper. For some reason, I trail my hands over my buzzcut, my face and down my throat, as if I can feel the drugs on my skin.

She shakes her head and silky hair slips over her slim shoulders as she clasps her hands in front of her as if in prayer. "You have to help me."

I shake my head, my body humming like a thousand bees under my skin. Her eyes, big, doe-shaped, lined with thick lashes, are the last things I see before I turn and sprint away as fast as I can.

Read the rest of the Bulwark Anthology!

Bulwark by Brit Lunden

The Knowing, Volume 1 by Brit Lunden

The Illusion, Volume 2 by DJ Cooper

The Craving, Volume 3 by R.L. Jackson

The Window, Volume 4 by E.H. Graham

The Missing Branch, Volume 5 by Kay MacLeod

The Body, Volume 6 by Kate Kelley

The Battle of Bulwark, Volume 7 by Del Henderson III

The Darkness, Volume 8 by Brittney Bass

If you enjoyed this story, please leave a review on Amazon, Goodreads, or wherever else you love to talk about books. Thank you!

Printed in Poland
by Amazon Fulfillment
Poland Sp. z o.o., Wrocław

50691683R00068